The McGraw-Hill Guide
to Electronic Research
in Theater

Diane Wienbroer

William Allen

Julie Booth

Boston   Burr Ridge, IL   Dubuque, IA   Madison, WI   New York   San Francisco   St. Louis
Bangkok   Bogotá   Caracas   Lisbon   London   Madrid
Mexico City   Milan   New Delhi   Seoul   Singapore   Sydney   Taipei   Toronto

McGraw-Hill Higher Education
A Division of The McGraw·Hill Companies

Published by McGraw-Hill, an imprint of the McGraw-Hill Companies, Inc., 1221 Avenue of the Americas, New York, NY 10020. Copyright © 2001 by the McGraw-Hill Companies, Inc. All rights reserved.

1 2 3 4 5 6 7 8 9 0 BKM/BKM 0 9 8 7 6 5 4 3 2 1 0

ISBN 0-07-236838-1

C O N T E N T S

P R E F A C E

This guide is for you if you are new to using the computer for research, or if you are an experienced computer user who now has to write a college term paper. Included in this guide are some suggestions for using the computer to ease your research and the reporting of it. Even though this guide is aimed at the writer of the research paper, student directors, student playwrights, student designers in scenery, costumes, lighting, and sound, and student performers can all benefit from knowing how to use the computer for project research.

You will succeed if you understand the nature of electronic research before you begin. Take some time now to skim over the various headings in each chapter. To make the best use of your time, read Chapters 1 and 2 before turning to the computer. By design there are portions of this booklet you may be able to skim, or skip altogether. Key terms are in **boldface**.

Once you begin your research, keep this guide handy while you are working at the computer. Internet addresses are listed throughout the book, and tips on using search engines are included in Chapter 3.

As you are gathering research for your project, use Chapter 4 to help you start an electronic archive and organize your research materials.

When you are ready to write your paper, or present your project, use Chapter 5 to supplement any directions your teacher or advisor has given you.

We hope that you find this guide useful. All Internet addresses in this guide are current as of July 2000. If you have questions, comments, or suggestions for revision, please e-mail or write us:

theater@mcgraw-hill.com

Theater Editor
McGraw-Hill College Division
Two Penn Plaza, 20th Floor
New York, NY 10121-2298

What You Need to Know before You Start

It's exciting and easy to search for information using computers—often to the point that it doesn't feel like work at all. However, it can also be frustrating and time consuming if you don't know what to expect. If you're new to computers—or if you're familiar with only one system—read this chapter before you start.

Information is available via computer in several ways:

- From home if you have an encyclopedia or other resource on CD-ROM, or have access to the Internet.
- At a library where you can consult the catalog as well as other databases installed in designated computers; you may also have Internet access at designated computers.
- At a college computer lab with Internet access.
- At a commercial outlet (perhaps called "Internet Cafe" or "Cyberhouse") where you can use computers for an hourly fee—check the Yellow Pages of your local directory under "Computer Rental" or "Computer Training." These places ordinarily have technical advisers, and may offer classes in using the Internet.

Note that even though the outlet may offer access to online commercial services, you can't use one without your own established personal account.

Definitions: Some key terms

A **CD-ROM** is a disk that looks just like an audio CD, but it contains computer programs or data—often the equivalent of whole shelves of books or periodicals. CD-ROM versions of encyclopedias, dictionaries, atlases, and other reference works are available in libraries and also for consumer purchase. Sometimes you are connecting to a CD-ROM on the Internet. *ROM* means "Read Only Memory" since the data on a CD-ROM is fixed (can't be changed), unlike the fluidity of information you encounter online.

Online is the term for being connected to another computer. You are not online when you are using a non-networked computer for reading a CD-ROM or word processing. The term *online* means that the computer you are using is communicating with another computer, for example, to connect to the Internet, or to access a library's regularly updated catalog and other resources.

The **Internet** is the name given to the network of all the computers in the world that can communicate with each other. The most common ways of communicating on the Internet are e-mail, telnet, FTP, gopher, newsgroups, and the World Wide Web.

Some of the computers on the Internet contain huge storehouses of information organized for easy public retrieval. Others (such as a university mainframe computer or America Online) provide the interconnections for networks of personal computers. Still other computers on the Internet provide information from businesses, government agencies, or nonprofit organizations. Connecting to the Internet allows you access to libraries and museums, computer software, elaborate graphics, and ads for products you may or may not want. Further, you can reach thoughtful and generous people who will respond to your questions or entertain you. Unfortunately, you may also encounter people who give misinformation or waste your time.

Via the Internet, you have access to all these resources—almost all of them for free. The challenge is to figure out which ones you want to connect to and how to do so efficiently. Once connected, you'll find some of the information presented in simple text format (plain black typeface on an unadorned screen), but you'll also find some valuable information festooned with colorful and entertaining artwork (including commercials), sound effects, video, and music.

Occasionally, you'll be asked to **register**—giving your name, address, and e-mail address. You will be told if fees are involved, but sometimes registration alone is necessary before you can read the information at that location.

The fastest growing area of the Internet is that of the **World Wide Web (WWW)**. This is the name for the **interlinked** part of the Internet where you can, with one keystroke, jump from one topic—and location—to another. You may have already seen this linking method if you've used a multimedia CD-ROM. As you scroll through the text, you encounter underlined and colored words or phrases; when you click your mouse (or press the Enter/Return key) on that phrase, you jump to a different page relevant to that topic.

Websites (locations on the World Wide Web) use this same linking method. Multimedia Websites also include audio (giving, for example, the pronunciation of a word) or video (a film clip). You might start looking at the **home page** (the first page of a Website) of the National Register of Historic Places at the U.S. Department of the Interior; then you might jump from there to a list of landmarked buildings; next you could see a picture of a specific building—all with just a few mouse clicks! Later, you might wonder how you got there, but the computer program allows you to go back to each previous screen, where each of the phrases you clicked on (**links**) will have changed color, so you can almost always retrace your path to the beginning of your session.

Another way people use the Internet is to send **e-mail** (electronic mail). This is the method of sending messages via computer, either to one person or to a group of people, once you know the correct Internet address. Computers make it possible to send copies simultaneously to a great many people, allowing for "live chats," where individuals type messages back and forth—and many others can read those messages, either at that time or later.

The most important characteristic of the Internet and more specifically the World Wide Web is openness: Anyone with the equipment and know-how can have a WWW page, and anyone else can read that page. Consequently, the Internet is accessible, democratic—and disorganized. Computers speed up access to information, but you can't predict what you will find. You may follow a promising lead and find notes from a scholarly seminar on your topic—or just as easily find someone's family portrait or rambling travelogue. Thus you need to be prepared to spend time searching for what you want.

Download is the term for copying a document from the Internet to your disk or the hard drive of your computer. We speak of computers as **loading** data from a disk or another computer. Thus a Webpage is loading onto your computer as it gradually comes into view. The computer where the Website is located (its **server**) is **uploading** the **Webpages** to you. Should you choose to save them, you would then download copies of those pages onto your own disk.

Note: Some college programs or libraries restrict the types of downloads you are allowed to do. You may be able to copy to your disk or print copies of the screens you are viewing, but you might not. You may also be restricted from downloading from commercial services, where fees could be involved. Be sure to ask where you are using the Internet what rules apply.

Be careful: If you do decide to download for a fee, make sure that your credit card number will be encrypted (scrambled). If it is not, you will be warned that you are about to submit an "insecure" document. If that is the case, others would be able to read your number. By law, a telephone number must be given so that you can phone in your order. Always read the "privacy statement" offered on the webpage if you are paying a fee.

If you have a sizable research project, you will want to save as much information as possible onto your disk (to avoid needless typing). Thus, when you go to the library or computer lab, plan to take several 3.5" disks formatted for the system used there (if you know whether it is Mac or PC). Then give a separate name to each document you copy to disk, so you can find it later.

Browse is the term for moving from one Website to another. Special software, a Web **browser** (such as Mosaic or Netscape), makes it possible for you to reach a Website by typing in its address or clicking on a highlighted phrase in a Web page. Time spent visiting a number of Websites is also called **surfing**—a good metaphor for the rapid movement that is possible on the Web.

▼ Connecting to the Internet

Even if you do not own computer or have an account with an Internet service provider (ISP), it is easy to have free access to the Internet through your college or university, or even your public library.

It is commonplace for libraries (community, public school, college, and university) to have computers that are connected to the Internet. These libraries typically allow user access for Internet browsing and have trained research librarians on-hand to help users begin their search. Most colleges and universities are wired to the Internet and have open computer labs where students can do online research. Another good resource for help and information about connecting to the Internet can be found through your college or university's Academic Computing or Information Service department.

Regardless of where you connect to the Internet, the computer you use is communicating (via modem or hard wire) with a powerful computer (the server) that is in turn connected to the Internet. From your personal computer or campus workstation, you use computer software that communicates with the server computer. (Ordinarily, that software is provided when you get an Internet account at home—either with your college or with a commercial service). Other software programs in the server allow you to use e-mail (electronic mail), browse the Web, or download files from the Internet to your disk. Because you are dealing with a server between you and the Internet, high usage may tax the system you are using; depending on how powerful the system is, you may have occasional or even frequent slowdowns—particularly at term paper times!

Equipment needed to connect to the Internet

If you want to use the Internet from home, you will need:

- A computer with at least 16 megabytes of memory.
- A modem (at least 28,800 speed) plus communications software to use it.
- A phone line (or a hard wire connection if your college provides it).
- Additional software depending on what your Internet server requires.

Optional equipment recommended for the World Wide Web includes:

- A color monitor.
- A sound card (already built into the Macintosh) and multimedia software if you want to use multimedia sources.

Internet accounts: Username and password

When you open an Internet account—either with your college or with a commercial online service—you will be asked to submit a **username** and **password** so you can logon and receive e-mail. The username (**ID** or **userid**) plus your server's address will be your e-**mail address** on the Internet (usually *username@server address*, such as janed@aol.com). Sometimes you won't get your first choice of username because someone else is already using it, or because your server assigns usernames by an established system.

Your password is the sequence of letters or numbers (or a combination of letters and numbers) that you type in to gain access to your account. Since you'll be using it often, select a password that is easy to remember and quick to type—and one that others won't be likely to guess. Be sure to type both your username and password carefully during the initial setup (because what you type is the only sequence the computer will recognize ever after) and write both down in a safe location (not in your computer files).

▼ Figuring out Internet addresses

The **Internet address** (sequence of letters and numbers you type to send e-mail or to reach another computer on the Internet) is based on an established system, DNS (Domain Name System). The last three digits designate the type of institution at the Internet address:

.edu is used by educational institutions
.org is used by nonprofit organizations
.gov is used by governmental agencies
.mil is used by the military
.com is used by commercial organizations
.net is used by large computer networks

These addresses assume that the site is in the United States. In addition, you may encounter addresses that end in a two-letter country code. Here are a few:

.at	Austria	.gr	Greece
.au	Australia	.il	Israel
.br	Brazil	.it	Italy
.ca	Canada	.jp	Japan
.ch	Switzerland	.kr	Korea
.de	Germany	.mx	Mexico
.es	Spain	.uk	United Kingdom
.fr	France	.us	United States

You can often figure out an unknown address by trying possible usernames with the proper suffix. For example, you can accurately deduce how to send an e-mail message on the Internet to the President of the United States:

president@whitehouse.gov

In addition, all the people in your system share the same address, so you can send messages to them once you know (or figure out) their usernames.

Besides using the Internet for e-mail, you will want to visit Websites. You reach sites on the World Wide Web by typing their addresses called **URLs** (universal resource locators), usually starting with http://www. See pages 42–45 for some important addresses, including directories to the Internet.

You can also figure out some addresses for World Wide Web sites. Try a simple name with the appropriate prefix and suffix. For example, you can reach these Websites by typing their fairly obvious addresses:

New York Times	http://www.nytimes.com
Wall Street Journal	http://www.wsj.com
Playbill	http://www.playbill.com
National Public Radio	http://www.npr.org
Yale University	http://www.yale.edu

Be careful: When typing, you must use the exact sequence of letters and of the address. Unlike a wrong number on the telephone, you won't know if our e-mail message reached the wrong person on the Internet. If you get a "404 error," "wrong DNS," or "unknown URL," check your typing first; if the spelling is correct, try one of the directories listed on pages 42–45. Be aware, however, that one of the most important characteristics of the Internet is its rapid rate of change. Most sites that move leave a forwarding address, but some do not.

▼ Getting around within different programs

Even if you've used a computer for word processing, you may encounter computer systems where your actions will not bring about the expected results. Regardless of the program you're using on your own computer, you will be restricted to the format of the program you're communicating with on the Internet.

Maneuvering with either keyboard or mouse

Selecting

Often you will tell the computer what you want by choosing from a **menu** (list) of options, or by **selecting** an underlined phrase presented in a different color from the rest of the text. You communicate your selection by clicking the mouse or by pressing Enter/Return after the choice is highlighted. Note that a phrase can't be selected until the cursor is positioned *exactly* on the phrase. With many programs, the cursor changes from an arrow to a hand pointing upward to indicate that you can select at that point.

Scrolling

Whether using a keyboard or mouse-based system, you **scroll** down (move vertically down through the text) as you read the material on the screen. For scrolling, you can use the arrow keys, the Page Up or Page Down keys, or the mouse. To use the mouse, look at the right edge of the screen. You will notice a vertical border for the window you are working in. If there are two borders, the one on the inner frame controls the window you're working in. You either position the cursor and click continuously on an arrow pointing in the direction you want to move the text (up or down), or you may click on a square "button" to slide it down the margin as you read. Just click and hold the mouse button down as you guide the mouse smoothly and in a straight line (toward you to go down; away from you to go up). This method is particularly useful if you want to skim a document quickly.

You won't be able to scroll through or save a document while it is loading. Programs usually provide a visual clue to the status of downloading—for example, a horizontal bar graph, a thermometer, shooting stars (Netscape), or a spinning pyramid (America Online).

Note: The position of the square "button" in the right margin is also a clue to the length of the material you are reading, since most of the time the pages aren't numbered. It will be at the top at the beginning of the document and all the way at the bottom at the end.

Saving

In nearly every program, the top of the screen will have a section labeled Options or Commands. Mouse-click (or arrow and press Enter/Return) to read a menu of choices. **Save** or **Record** will allow you to save the data in the file on your current screen (which you can then read more carefully and extract specific notes from) and may even give an appropriate footnote.

Even if you routinely save to your hard drive, always back up your files on a floppy disk.

Insert your formatted disk into the computer. Be sure to name each file with a different name, and write down the full title and Internet address (you can't enter any of your own writing directly on this file yet).

Note: Only the file you're actually reading will be saved, not any of the linked files. If you want to save them also, you have to get each file on the screen and save each one separately.

If you are working in a library or computer lab, be sure to save your notes in text-only format, both to save space and to make sure that your word processing program can read them. Some libraries or computer labs may not allow you to save on your own disk. If not, see whether you can print the files you want.

Other options

The headings in each program vary, but there are usually a number of useful options listed on the top of the screen. If you highlight them there will either be an explanation or a drop-down menu. Just mouse-click on the heading. Then, while holding the mouse button down, drag down to highlight your choice and release the mouse. See the inside back cover for definitions of the **Bookmark, Reload, Forward, Back, Stop,** and **History** buttons.

Error messages

Many programs will alert you with a sound effect if you're trying to perform something that won't work. Others will give an error message. You can usually click on **Help** to learn what to do.

Exiting

As you enter a program, often there will be a line at the beginning telling you how to exit or quit. Note that command (frequently Alt + F4). If you forget, you can usually type Q or mouse-click in the top-right or top-left corner where you'll see an X or square. **Don't just turn off your computer**— particularly if you're connected to a text-based host computer program. It can leave that computer line busy for others.

Preparing for Your Research

Using computers to find information sounds easy, and often it is. However, you will also have access to much more material than you could ever read, and the information you need may be buried under a lot of stuff you don't care about. Researching with computers can be successful only when you understand how the information is organized, as well as what computers can and cannot do.

What computers can and cannot do

Whether you are searching on CD-ROM or on the Internet, **search tools** (computer programs that locate sources of information) will ask you for a subject area or for search terms (keywords). Researching programs are user friendly, so you'll often get plenty of information quickly. However, you still need to be creative in how you tell the computer what to look for.

What Computers Can Do	*What You Must Do*
Scan a vast number of documents rapidly	Determine the best words to use for scanning the documents
Organize the results	Indicate your priorities
Respond to your specific limits	Articulate those limits
Allow you to download files to use in your report	Save the files on your disk; record bibliographic information

What Computers Cannot Do	*What You Must Do*
Find something wrapped inside something else	Use synonyms; suggest more general topics; be creative in phrasing your search
Find something that isn't there	Recognize that some material isn't available electronically; understand how files are stored; carefully select the databases you search
Correct a misspelled word	Proofread zealously; use alternate spelling when appropriate; recognize that typos occur in indexes and catalogs
Discriminate between different meanings, such as Mercury the car or planet and mercury the mineral	Add words preceded by "not" so you eliminate unwanted usage of your search term
Provide context	Add terms that provide context, such as "classical Greek tragedy"

Understanding where the information is

Although computers have revolutionized the way libraries work, the basic method of organizing resources remains the same as that of the old print-based days: Librarians catalog books, magazines, newspapers, photographs, and recordings by author, title, and subject, with cross-references to important subtopics within the subject. This information is stored in the library's **catalog,** so you can look for a work by subject—or by author or title if you have that information. Articles in magazines and newspapers are listed in **indexes** according to this same method. Computer programs can rapidly scan catalogs and indexes—even pages of articles or the tables of contents and indexes of individual books—for words you specify. Some programs also look for related subtopics that you haven't even mentioned. In addition, electronic databases can sometimes give you the text itself to read on the screen or to print out.

Databases

Academic research papers require information found in articles published in scholarly periodicals, many of which are not on the Web. Therefore, you will need to consult some **specialized databases** that index scholarly articles. There are four types of specialized databases: bibliographic and full-text databases, statistical sources, and directories. Your library will have a number of these installed in designated computers for you to consult.

Bibliographic databases (lists of titles of books and articles) are the most common type of database. These indexes and catalogs will usually give you a brief description or the abstract of a book or article, along with the title, author, publisher, date of publication, and number of pages.

In the library, you will have access not only to its catalog but also to a variety of indexes on CD-ROM, installed at designated computers. You can find out which periodicals the library subscribes to in the catalog, but to find specific articles, you will need to consult indexes. For example, you can find general interest magazines and newspapers indexed in the *Magazine Index* or the *Readers' Guide to Periodical Literature.*

Journals useful for theater history, dramaturgy, and period styles, are covered by *Art Abstracts, Humanities Abstracts, International Bibliography of Theatre, MLA Bibliography,* and the *Dissertation Abstracts International.* Some of these indexes are available for limited searching at the Getty Research Institute: http://www.getty.edu/gri (click on "Research Library").

One of the most useful indexes is the *Arts and Humanities Citation Index*, which indexes footnotes and bibliographies from scholarly journals. If you are writing a research paper on modern American theater and have found a useful article by Robert Brustein, you could look up his name and the title of his article in the citation index to find pointers to other writers who have referenced the article. The print version of the *Arts and Humanities Citation Index* covers publications since 1975.

After finding the titles of books and articles you want to read, you'll then have to find them in the library. The database will often tell you the location of the book or article—whether it's in the reference section, on reserve, on microfilm or microfiche.

Full-text databases include the whole text, not just the title. Understandably, there are not very many of these, and they usually present only sources from the last few years. Most of these indexes provide unformatted texts for recent articles, but the Bartleby and Gutenberg projects on the Web have scanned entire books in beautiful format. If you want, you can read these books on the screen. On the Internet, some full-text databases require a fee for you to see the actual text. However, selected recent articles are available free from *Early Modern Literary Studies* (http://purl.oclc.org/emls/emlshome.html), *The New York Times* Arts/Living section (http://www.nytimes.com), and *Theater Journal* (http://muse.jhu.edu/journals/theatre_journal/). Ken McCoy at Stetson University maintains a Website of online resources for Theater and Performance Studies. McCoy's Website can be found at http://www.stetson.edu/departments/csata/thr_guid.html.

▼   **The Internet**

In addition to the library with its books, journals, and electronic databases, you have the entire Internet to explore. Since 1987, people all over the world, usually as part of their jobs or schoolwork, have been scanning in titles, summaries, and even entire copies of articles and books, creating lists of resources, writing informative studies—and putting the results up on the World Wide Web for everyone to freely use. See, for example, the UCLA Arts Library Website, http://www.library.ucla.edu/libraries/arts/websites/wwwthea.htm, for a comprehensive list of performance related resources.

Of particular interest to theater historians and students of period styles is the development of excellent Websites dedicated to art and architecture resources. Some sites in these categories are Washington's National Gallery of Art (http://www.nga.gov), *Didaskalia: Ancient Theatre Today* (http://didaskalia.berkeley.edu), and *Period and Style for Designers* by Hugh Lester at Tulane (http://www.tulane.edu/lester/text/lester.html).

▼ Expect to use printed sources

Most books and articles are not available online. You will still need to go to the library to read them and take notes. And you may prefer to read printed sources even when they are also available on computer.

- Most electronic texts of articles are devoid of formatting. You get just plain typeface—often many screenfuls—that you have to search carefully to find what you want. Formatting in print, on the other hand, makes it easy to skim material. You can read selected passages in a long article, noting headings, illustrations, and first and last paragraphs.
- You can browse in print, flipping through the table of contents or index of a book, for example, or sampling a middle chapter.
- It may be faster to find the print version. For example, even when you know that a particular article was on the front page of last Sunday's *New York Times*, you won't find the article nearly so fast electronically as you will if you just go to the library and pick up the paper, because only selected articles of the *New York Times* appear online, and what's available isn't indexed by page number.
- Text-only electronic versions of articles are taken out of the context of the original. Graphics, other articles, and advertisements adjacent to an article in a newspaper or journal can give you a broader sense of history and culture.
- You can immediately tell the size of a book or article in print, but it's difficult to get a sense of the length of some computerized texts. You won't necessarily know even when the size of the file is given (for example, 15K) because some of those kilobytes may be for graphics. (Without graphics, 15K is about six pages.) If the information is given, note the pages an article covered in its original form.

▼ **General guidelines for a research project**

The same guidelines for searching through print apply to researching electronically:

- Spend preliminary time jotting down ideas and questions.
- Determine the level of information you need and the time limits of your project.
- Continually refine your search as you go.
- Save notes on your computer disk when possible.
- Record the source of every fact or quotation.
- Stop periodically to assess your progress and write your thoughts on what you are discovering.
- Stay open to discovery, allowing time for browsing and reflection.

For example, if your topic is classical Greek theater, first narrow your topic by figuring out what you'd like to learn about. Are you interested in a specific Greek play? Would you like to find out about ancient costumes? Perhaps you are interested in the evolution of tragedy from the dithyramb. Reading a related chapter in your textbook or seeking out an article in an encyclopedia will give you some background. While you are reading, make a list of questions so that you can later extract keywords or terms for your search.

Listing associated subject areas where you might find information may be helpful (political history, religious history, art history, architecture, etc.) The Greek ministry of commerce might be a good source for images of the Theater Dionysus if you are researching theater architecture.

Even if you are very familiar with your topic, jot down an abstract of your paper so that when you discuss your paper with a librarian or your teacher, or post a question to a theater newsgroup, you will have some idea of the information you will be searching for.

Often it is difficult to plan a project or know what direction it will take until you do some initial research. Ideally, you should begin your research early so that you have the luxury of exploring and investigating all of your resources. Remember, always remain aware of the assignment and your level of expertise. What **level of information** do you need? A 20-page paper needs much more detailed attention than a 5-page paper. A paper on classical Greek tragedy will be much more complex and specific for a class in theater history than for theater appreciation.

▼ Time management

If you will be connecting to the Internet from home, don't forget to **allow time to use the library** where you'll need to consult print sources—and perhaps get a librarian's help.

With electronic research, you'll quickly get a great deal of information. Be sure to have a plan so you have time to **analyze** the researched material. Stop periodically to assess both the emerging general picture you have of your topic and the quality of the specific information. Researching electronically can become a mesmerizing activity, and you might find that at the end of a pleasant afternoon there is nothing to report. You might even try setting a timer (some computers have this feature installed), stopping every hour or so to make sure you have something concrete, so you aren't caught empty-handed at the deadline.

In libraries, you may be restricted to 15 minutes' usage of a computer during peak times. If you're using a commercial service, you can easily run up a huge bill. Here are some tips to most effectively use your time online:

- Narrow your search and have a good list of search words before you go online.
- Use the **helpline** (look for a button with a question mark or for Help or Search for Help), particularly when you use any program for the first time.
- Use **keywords** and the **Back** button; **bookmark** favorite sites (see typing reminders on the inside back cover).
- As you come across interesting information, save it to your disk and then read or print offline.
- Compose and read e-mail offline (your program will show you how).
- If a site takes too long to come up, use the Stop button at the top of the screen (or Ctrl + Pause, or Esc) to interrupt the request. Then make a note of it and try again later.
- If you are working on a computer with a fast processor, open several different browser windows at a time. If you are using a PC, you can right click on a link to have the option of opening in another window. On a Mac, click and hold down on the link to get the option to open in a new window. Opening several windows can be useful when you have a page of promising search-engine returns. Watch that your machine does not slow down by opening too many windows at once. Both Netscape and Internet Explorer have a function that lists a history of sites you have visited. You can always use this tool to return to your list of search results.

On the other hand, **recognize the value of browsing.** Allow time (say in half an hour) for aimless exploring. Since the Web is constantly changing, give yourself the chance to be open to new discoveries. If you feel overwhelmed or frustrated, stop to recall what you asked the computer to do. You may have asked the wrong question, or the answer you expect is not as readily available as you hoped. You need not be intimidated by the wealth of information on the Internet. You can, with patience, usually find ways to discover what you want to know.

A WORD ABOUT INTERNET COURTESY

Although the Internet often feels huge and impersonal, your behavior will affect other human beings. There are a few ground rules based on the spirit of the Internet.

- Communication between computers means you're using the time and energy (**bandwidth**) of other computers whenever you logon or connect to a Website. Don't tax the system by carelessly typing addresses; surfing areas you have no interest in; failing to logoff properly; or using a foreign site when a domestic one is available. When possible, download at offpeak times; when a site gives you the option, choosing to download at a high "niceness level" creates the least amount of site slowdown for other users.
- Honor the time limits on a library computer during peak usage. Empty your e-mail regularly. Cancel subscriptions to Listservs and Usent groups when your interest has waned.
- When visiting a newsgroup, read the FAQs (list of frequently asked/answered questions) first; then "lurk" for several days to learn the acceptable behavior for that group before commenting. This way, you'll get a sense of the intellectual level of the conversation, the philosophy of the majority of users, and the treatment of newcomers.
- You may have heard of "flaming"—an abusive or sarcastic response to a posting on the Internet. Some groups accept and even encourage such a tone, but many do not. It's best to be sure which group you're in.

C H A P T E R 3

Conducting
Your Research

Before you begin your research, you'll need a clear idea of what you want to discover. You may want just to browse first—either in your library or on the Internet. If you begin with a general subject, you may get plenty of information from whatever turns up first. By taking time to narrow your search you might get more specific information (closer to what you really want). In any case, you'll need some words to type in to tell the computer what you're looking for.

 ## Searching in your library

Your college or university library most likely has electronic resources. You can expect your library to have an electronic card catalog and some specialized databases available on CD-ROM or by license over the Internet. No matter what level of electronic resources your library has, it is always the best place to begin a research project. Take some time to familiarize yourself with your library's resources before beginning your project.

One major benefit for working in the library is that you will have trained human help if you need it. The majority of reference librarians are trained in search techniques on CD-ROM databases and in Internet resources. Many libraries offer quick seminars or tutorials in research techniques. It is to your advantage to use whatever library help is available.

When seeking help from a reference librarian, it is a good idea to have a list of information sources that you have already located. Not only will you impress your librarian with this demonstration of your attempts to find material on your own, you will save time by using the reference librarian's expertise in locating sources that are more difficult to find. Chances are that as you accumulate a list of titles that you want to see, some of these will not be immediately available in your library. All libraries have a cooperative agreement with other libraries for inter-library-loans. This service may take days or weeks to reach your library. This is another good reason to begin your research early!

   If your library has a good source of electronic databases that lead to journal articles, then you will want to take full advantage of this service. If your institution does not have access to journal article databases, this Web source could be of help: *UnCoverWeb* at http://uncweb.carl.org. You may search the site by title or subject. Searching is free; for a fee you can have the company fax or mail a photocopy of most articles to you. Full details are available on the Website. If you do find an item that is of interest, check to see if your library has it before you pay to have a copy sent to you.

 ## Searching in libraries elsewhere

Just as you can search for materials in your own library's electronic card catalog, you can search the electronic card catalogs of other libraries. Several universities and other institutions make their catalogs available over the Internet and even though you will not be able to borrow directly from the remote library, you can find all of the bibliographic information to pass on to your inter-library-loan service.

   Libraries with online catalogs available to the public often have excellent search facilities (by author, title, and subject). In addition, many have a mechanism in which you can mark items of interest and request the system to e-mail the bibliographic information to you. When you visit a remote library, carefully read the introductory material so you know how to use the system.

   Try the Library of Congress (http://LCweb.loc.gov) for its vast resources. The introductory materials "Using the Library" will help you figure out how to get the information you need. Other university research libraries with excellent resources are:

New York University	http://www.nyu.edu/library
Harvard University	http://hplus.harvard.edu (Hollis Library)
Boston University	http://web.bu.edu/library
University of California System	http://www.ucop.edu/ucophome/library.html
Indiana University	http://www.indiana.edu/~libweb/

Note that some library connections, especially those via Telnet, request that you "sign off" or "exit" when you are finished. This is important since libraries can only accommodate a limited number of visitors at a time, and if you leave without telling the system that you are leaving, your connection will remain open until it "times out."

Start with a broad topic heading: Greek architecture. Microsoft's *Bookshelf '98* gives an entry, Greek architecture and art, which offers a brief chronological survey of the major developments of Greek architecture from the Geometric through the Hellenistic periods. Some key terms (for example, *column, temple*, and *mural painting*) are highlighted as links to other articles in the CD-ROM. Listed beneath the main topic are references to some specific Greek buildings as well as ancillary topics such as Greek Revival. Jot down terms that look promising for use as you expand your search to other electronic resources. Like other modern CD-ROM reference works, *Bookshelf 2000* also lets you launch your keywords as searches on *Encarta Online* and on an Internet search engine.

Even though nothing that you find in such a general reference work (whether it be on CD-ROM or a hardbound desk encyclopedia) is likely to find its way into your final research, you will have spent very little time and accumulated several topical jumping-off points for further investigation in books, journals, and Internet sites.

With a topic such as Greek stagecraft, you will probably use more articles than books to get your information. However, check the library catalog, using the keywords for a subject search and the names of any experts you came across for a search by author (to see if your library has any books written by these experts).

Searching on the Internet

Searches on the World Wide Web are conducted primarily by computer programs called search engines. For the purpose of conducting online research, it is important to understand the difference between search engines and directories. Also called *spiders* or *crawlers*, **search engines** are programmed to visit web sites on the Internet in order to create catalogs of web pages. Unlike search engines, **directories** are created by humans. Sites are submitted to be assigned to an appropriate category. Since humans actually index these sites, directories can often provide more logically organized information than search engines. Some **hybrid** search engines also have an associated directory. These are directories of sites that have been reviewed and categorized by humans.

Searching engines, metasearch engines, and doing advanced searching

There are hundreds of search engines for use on the World Wide Web. Most people agree that seven major engines dominate the Web (AltaVista, Yahoo!, etc.). The search engine site *Search Engine Watch* (http://www.searchenginewatch.com) is a helpful resource in evaluating these sites.

Most students access the Web using Netscape or Internet Explorer. The simplest ways to get to the major search engines are by clicking on the Search button at the top of Internet Explorer or Netscape Communicator or by using the pull-down Directory in Netscape Navigator (use Internet Search). You can begin your search by choosing one of these major engines.

Another good way to test search engines is by using a **metacrawler** or **metasearch engine**. Unlike search engines, metacrawlers don't spider through Websites themselves to create catalogs. Instead, they send your search to a number of search engines all at once. The results are listed by search engine name. This can be helpful when you are determining which search engine is most likely to give you the kind of information you are looking for. Go2Net / MetaCrawler (http://www.go2net.com) is an example of a metasearch program. Search Engine Watch (mentioned above) also has a list of metacrawlers and metasearch engines on its site.

Regardless of what search engine you use, it is always a good idea to visit the help section. There you will find information on how to enter search words to help control the way the engine returns results to you. For example, the ability to tell AltaVista that you want *theater* but not *movie* (+ theater – movie) will eliminate a lot of movie sites that may have shown up otherwise. The ability to submit *theat** will let the engine find returns on both the American ("theater") or European ("theatre") spellings.

There are a variety of ways to limit your searches. Each engine has its own protocol and features, and each has its own "advanced search" help section that will aid you in refining your search. AltaVista, for example, supports image tag searching and will translate sites written in other languages. Spend some time researching the search engines to find the one that best suits your needs.

Directories

Directories are indexes of sites that are reviewed and indexed by humans. Yahoo! (http://www.yahoo.com) is the most widely used directory where the finds are indexed. At Yahoo! you can enter search terms and get returns; you can also follow the hierarchy of the Yahoo! index to find the subject or subjects you want. For theater students, the first Yahoo! category in the hierarchy is "Arts and Humanities." From there choose "Performing Arts," then "Theater." Here you will find various categories of "Theater" (Awards, Directing, History, Musicals, etc.) with the number of links indicated next to each listing. While what you find indexed in a directory may be only a superficial listing of what is available on the World Wide Web, generally using an index is a good way to locate sites as starting places for your research.

Hybrids

Searching with hybrid can be a good starting point using features from both directories and search engines. AskJeeves (http://askjeeves.com) is a hybrid search that attempts return the exact page that answers your question from a catalog indexed by humans. If it fails to find a match within its own catalog, AskJeeves functions like a metasearch engine and will provide matching Web pages from various search engines.

Theater-specific search engines

To date, there is no specific search engine for the theater. However, there are a number of directories to theater pages on the Web. Scott's Theatre Links (http://www.theatre-link.com) is one such example. The author of this page has created a directory of categorized links to sites specifically about theater. Although there is a search function on this site, at this writing, the search only looks through Scott's Theatre Links' database.

Many other directories of theater sites can be found on the Web. McCoy's Guide to Internet Resources in Theatre and Performance Studies (http://www.stetson.edu/ departments/csata/thr_guid.html) is an excellent directory that lists other theater site directories.

▼ What if there is no match for your request

- You may have misspelled one or more words.
- You may have used the wrong symbols or phrasing for that particular search engine. Check the directions or helpline.
- You may have submitted too narrow a search. Try generalizing a bit—for example change the phrase "staging in classical Greek tragedy" to "Greek tragedy."
- Give the abbreviation and the full name, linked by *or—for example "RNT or Royal National Theatre."*
- The information may be at a location that is either down or experiencing heavy usage.
- Your computer server may be experiencing a slow-down—again due to heavy usage.

▼ What if you get too many listings?

- Take a look at the first 10 to see if they coincide at all with your topic. For instance, if your inquiry on the Globe yielded thousands of articles, and the first 10 are all about the earth, you'll need to rephrase the search string.
- If the first 10 listings *are* on your topic, download a few of them to skim offline, and extract more search terms to use.
- Add more words to your search string. Try putting a more specific word first:

    Globe + theatre + Shakespeare + performances

When possible, link (+) the terms so that all will appear in your selected documents.

Assessment questions

If you encounter an author or title repeatedly as you research among scholarly publications, you'll have an indication of which authorities are the most respected. On the other hand, the number of accessions (or "hits") of a particular Website will indicate its popularity, but what is hot is not necessarily the most reliable. You will always need to assess the quality of the information.

Note the Internet address of the source. Is it commercial (i.e., does the address end in .com)? That may not be inappropriate in itself, but just as there is a difference between magazines and scholarly journals, there is a difference between a document on a commercial Website and a paper posted by an educational, governmental, or nonprofit organization. Be prepared to get additional evidence or support.

Some of the most useful sites for theater students are these maintained by theater scholars. Scholars offer two types of Websites. The first type is the research project that resides on the Web. For example, Rob Shakespeare, noted lighting designer and faculty member from the Theatre Department at Indiana University, is researching the potential uses of computers in lighting design. The ongoing results of his research are documented at http://www.cica.indiana.edu/ projects/theatre. Many noted scholars at major research institutions are publishing their research on the Web, making valuable information available with just a few clicks of the mouse.

The second type of scholarly sites are online research guides and linked review sites created for theater students. An example of this kind of site can be found at many college and university theater home pages. See for example, University of Washington Professor Jack Wolcott's "Theatre History on the Web" page (http://www.artsci.washington.edu/drama/jack.html).

How do you determine a scholarly form an unscholarly site?

First, as you do searches, be on the lookout for returns that point to sites whose addresses end in .edu (education) or .org (nonprofit organizations such as NPR). Second, look for sites that do not have a large number of banner ads. Advertisements on a site tend to indicate that the site is more commercial in nature. This does not mean that some commercial sites (Playbill Online, for example) will not have scholarly information; but it should indicate that a more thorough assessment is necessary. Third, look for the credentials of the author. Most reputable sites will give a short biography of the author, for example, "Julie Booth, M.F.A., Assistant Professor, Theatre Design and Technology, West Virginia University is a recipient of the Academic Computing Faculty Research Grant." Most authors include an e-mail address on their site. A good tactic for finding other scholarly sites is to contact the author and ask him or her to recommend other scholarly sources.

As you find reliable sources on the Internet and gather information about your topic, you still have the task of deciding which resources will help you move forward in your research and which might need to be put aside for another project. List the categories for the information you have accumulated. Arrange a simple outline (or a topic "tree" with subtopic "branches"). Consider how topics could be further subdivided. Note the names of experts or areas you want to pursue—and those you want to drop. Finally, what conclusions does the information suggest?

After reviewing your notes, do some freewriting to see if you can identify the main points and where the holes in facts and the gaps in reasoning are. Rarely is one search session adequate, even for a short research project. Follow up on the subtopics or expert names in the same search engines or databases you were using.

 Searching the Internet for other sources

Home pages of colleges and universities

More and more college faculty use the Internet as part of their courses. Through the searching techniques already described, you may have already encountered syllabi or reading lists that will help you in your research. In addition, try searching with terms from the academic course appropriate to your topic.

Websites of governmental and other nonprofit organizations

Check the directories or search engines (pp. 42–45) to find Websites of organizations devoted to your subject area. Often the links will lead you to alternate sources of information. For example, National Public Radio covers many topics—current affairs, politics, the economy, the arts, and science. Tapes or transcripts of broadcasts are available, for a fee, or you may listen to the broadcasts over the internet for no charge.

Using a gopher

This is an easy way to find sites on the Internet. Gopher is a menu system, meaning that you have a list of choices to select, connecting you each time to research facilities appropriate to the subject you specify. The name is a tribute both to the mascot at the University of Minnesota where the system was developed, and to the speed of its fast retrieval ("go-for"). Type *gopher://gopher.tc.umn.edu* to start your search, then click on the libraries you are interest in.

Type in the general subject and get a list of related sites—most of which are university libraries. You then click on the one you want and go directly to it.

Note that the gopher is a simple, nongraphic searcher. This means that it often can get results faster than the search engines because it bypasses complex graphics, but this also means it will miss many sites on the Web. It is, however, a faster way to find research libraries, and a favorite among people using a slow modem.

Using Telnet

Telnet is an established method of communicating on the Internet, but unlike the other older methods, it hasn't been replaced by other functions on the World Wide Web. At this writing, many libraries and usergroups are only available through Telnet, so you may find that you have to tackle this technology. Basically, it is the protocol (system of computer rules and formats) that allows you to communicate directly with another, distant computer. The technology allows your keyboard to behave as if it were attached to the other computer and its programs.

For Mac and Windows users, using Telnet, which is UNIX based, is not easy. Not only is the mouse useless, touching it can sometimes even break the connection. Also, keystrokes may produce very different results from what the label on the key says. For example, an arrow key may add an unremovable symbol. If your library or computer lab does not provide detailed written instructions, ask a librarian or technical staff member for help.

First, determine if you have Telnet on your system. (Colleges with UNIX do; other systems—including commercial online servers—may require that you install additional software.)

Get the Telnet address. You usually encounter one when you're on a Website and want to go further, but you may also find what you want at http://www.einet.net/. Write down the address and also the *exact* letters of the **logon** (letters that you type in to start the program)—usually a word in all capitals. You may also be given a password and the **logoff** (letters that you type to exit the program).

At the prompt line or the Telnet window of your program, type in the address—the name of the organization or a series of numbers, like a phone number, separated by periods.

When you reach the site, you'll first be conscious of its simple look—just plain typeface. You may need to adjust the screen size; check the top of the screen for Options. Read the initial directions and write down (if one is given) the **escape character**—usually three keyboard symbols, such as +++, that you must use when you give commands at this site. If you don't have it already, write down the logoff to type in for the end of your session.

Type in the required logon, and follow scrupulously the directions on the screen. Don't touch any keys until you are instructed to do so. Be sure to type slowly, allowing for the brief time lag it takes for your keystroke to communicate with the other computer. If you make a mistake in typing, you can either Backspace/Delete to fix it or press Enter/Return and usually the program will allow you to retype.

Be sure to logoff once you have finished. Logoff is *{/}QUIT*.

To solve some common Telnet problems, try the following approaches:

- If the site asks you what kind of terminal you have, try pressing Enter/Return. If the site repeats the question, try entering *VT100* (the most common terminal type) according to the directions on the screen.
- If you forget the logoff or it doesn't seem to work, press */]/* or *Q*.
- Type *?* or *H* for help.

Using e-mail

Newsgroups (Usenet)

People communicate regularly on the Internet, and some are highly knowledgeable about the subject being discussed. One way to get in on the conversation is to read the postings on a **BBS** (bulletin board server) or **newsgroup** (a forum devoted to a particular topic, on which people send in their comments by e-mail). However, for research purposes, you need to be cautious. Anyone can claim to be an authority; be prepared to check a second source to back up what you get from a newsgroup.

Although you can't expect these forums to do your research for you, you will get useful information if you select your group well. Be sure to allow enough time to follow a discussion over several weeks.

You may have heard of real-time conversations (live chat) on the Internet. The online services organize a number of chat rooms on various topics; see page 44–45 for addresses for others.

The fastest way to get information from news groups is to use **Dejanews Research Service** (http://www.dejanews.com), which allows you to search for a specific topic (thread) previously discussed in all newsgroups—or those you specify. This way you don't have to wait for e-mail, and you don't have to search the archives of the individual newsgroups. Dejanews allows for quite a sophisticated query, so you can specify dates or even the university addresses of those who post. The service also gives good advice on how to conduct a search.

The only drawback is that Dejanews lists results in reverse chronology (the latest is listed first), so although you get the best match for your search terms on the top of the list, you are reading answers to earlier communications (which you haven't read yet). Nevertheless, this is a more efficient way to track down information from this source—rather than searching through the archives of each newsgroup one at a time.

Mailing lists (Listserv)

If you have a long-term research project, you may decide to join a mailing list where you can get all the group's messages sent to your e-mail address.

There are organized mailing lists on almost any topic. You can join one of these e-mail conferences by merely sending a message to the organizer.

Be careful: You may get a flood of e-mail. Select your list carefully and cancel when you are no longer interested.

First, select a list. You can search a list of descriptions and addresses at

http://www.liszt.com

or

http://stetson.edu/departments/csta/thr_guid.html (see "Listservs")

There are two types of lists: moderated (where a person or committee selects which messages will be posted to the group) and unmoderated (where the computer sends all messages out to the group, regardless of content). Some groups also sort messages by content (threads), so you can read only those messages that interest you.

If your e-mail program doesn't subscribe you automatically, you'll need to print out and save the directions to subscribe and (most important) to unsubscribe. **Listsev** is the program which manages the subscription to mailing lists.

Note: There are always two addresses—one to subscribe or unsubscribe (the address with *serv* in it), and one to address messages to the group (usually *group@its address*). Don't confuse the two. Because computers blindly process your e-mail message, it's as useless to tell the whole group of subscribers to unsubscribe you as it is to give your remarks on an important topic to the computer that is composing the subscription list.

Submit a request to subscribe by sending an e-mail message according to the directions. Usually, you leave the subject line blank. In the body, you give your real name and e-mail address and add the line *subscribe.*

If you can, specify a summary or digest form. (The directions will tell you if that is possible; often you specify that only after you are already a subscriber.) The digest form means that you'll get summaries of the messages—an advantage when there are many responses each day, as there sometimes are.

When you're finished with your project, be sure to unsubscribe, sending the appropriate message, as given in the initial directions. Usually, this is the same message as your first one, with the substitution of the word *unsubscribe* for the word *subscribe,* sent to the subscription address.

Query by e-mail

You may already have enough information to sift through, but often a direct question to a person can be the fastest way to get a good perspective on your topic. You might want to try a direct question to a known expert in the area of your research. To discover Internet addresses for the names of people encountered in your research whom you'd like to interview, consult one of the Internet directories (see pp. 42–45). Of course, many individuals don't answer "cold calls" queries, but a respectful, carefully phrased, and intelligent question might yield a response.

General advice for e-mail

You may get answers to your questions by reviewing the FAQs (Frequently Asked Questions) or the **archives** (previous messages or postings sent), available through Dejanews (p. 28) or listed when you subscribe. Be sure to read both for a few days before sending an e-mail query yourself. You'll invite negative responses if you ask a question that is redundant or inappropriate. Since some mailing lists are really scholarly conferences by e-mail, check carefully before attempting to participate.

As you scroll through a list of messages in a newsgroup, you'll notice the importance of accurate wording for the subject line. A well-phrased subject line assures that the message will be read by people who are interested in that topic. Many people ignore messages with vague or emotional subject lines (such as "I need help!"). Give a concise indication of your message: "Request anecdotes on theater period styles research papers."

You will also notice that some people repeat the entire message they're responding to, since some e-mail programs make it easy to do so. It's preferable to quote briefly from the message you're responding to, using an angle bracket (>) on each line to indicate the quote. Some e-mail programs do this automatically. In addition, avoid sending nonsubstantial messages such as "I agree." Reply only when you can contribute to the conversation.

Knowing when to stop your search

The problem most researchers encounter is in gauging how much time to allow for the search and for the report. One thing you can count on is that writing the report almost always will take much longer than you expect. Since with computers you can write and research intermittently, add your thoughts as you assemble the notes from your electronic sources. Allow time for reflection—and for additional research if you discover gaps in your information.

CHAPTER   C H A P T E R   **4**

Organizing and Archiving Your Research

▼ **Starting your own digital archive**

As you collect materials for your research project, you may want to maximize the use of your computer by organizing your research materials and storing them in a digital archive. Storing everything on the computer (notes, downloaded Web pages, bibliography, digital images, etc.) means that when the time comes to put your project together, everything is in the same place. The following are some tips for storing your research materials on disk and on your computer. Remember, always back up your research on disk!

Bookmarks

If you own your own computer, learn to use bookmarks effectively on your Web browser. If you are viewing a website, you can add **bookmarks** (Netscape) or **favorites** (Internet Explorer) to your browser preference file. The next time you want to visit the page, "pull down" your bookmarks (or favorites) and click on the title page you want to revisit—the browser will reconnect to the site automatically.

Note: In your browser preferences, you have the option of choosing whether to download the page from its originating server or from the computer's cache memory. If you are dealing with large files (such as images) on a static site that will not change, you may want to retrieve your bookmark from the cache so that you will save download time.

Organizing your bookmarks makes it easier to locate something that you know you once marked. How you organize your bookmarks should depend on how you want to use them. Generally, it is a good idea to create a task folder, naming it something that relates to your project, for example: Theater History Paper. Within Theater History Paper create subfolders such as: Good Links, Scholarly Essays, Picture Sources, and so forth, so that you can easily find a site weeks after you've marked it. Your browser will allow you to reorganize your bookmarks as your research progresses.

Text Materials

If you are consolidating your research and writing materials on the computer, you will have several kinds of text: notes taken from print and electronic sources, bibliographic information, drafts of your paper, and perhaps some e-mail messages related to your project. Try to keep all of your text in compatible file formats as you move from one computer to another. Saving files as "Text Only" (with a .txt extension) will allow you to view them on DOS, Windows, and Mac machines.

E-mail messages can usually be saved in plain text or HTML (Web Page style), depending on how they were composed and how they were received by your e-mail program. It is a good idea to keep the "pure extract" of the e-mail in your archive. When you are quoting from an e-mail message in a scholarly paper, check the formatting so that the message reads smoothly—either as a short quotation or as indented text for longer messages.

Keep project materials together in a format that is similar to the way you have organized your bookmarks. Create a project folder and then create subfolders to hold different types of materials.

The **bibliography** is a special situation. The practice of keeping a complete bibliographic reference file with a shorthand notation for each reference in your notes is a good procedure. Some scholars use specialized bibliographic software to store their records. The advantage of this software is that it allows the user to store information in discreet categories (author, title, year, etc.) and then produces both foot- or endnotes and bibliographies in any number of different styles (MLA, Chicago Manual style, etc.). The user can also tag each entry with keywords by which the items can be easily retrieved.

Some word processors have built-in bibliographic "wizards" that help with the construction of notes and bibliographies. Some people prefer to keep their bibliographies in a spreadsheet or database. The advantage to bibliographic software, whether purchased or designed by you in a database program, is that your gathering form will have blanks for all the information needed for a *complete* reference. (See Chapter 5 for more detailed bibliographic and citation styles.)

Images

If you are writing a paper on theater history or period styles of the theater, images may play a role in your research. Just as you collect notes taken from Web pages, journals, and so forth, and file them, you might wish to save images for use in your final paper.

A note about copyright: Many of the images that you find in print, or as part of a digital medium (CD-ROM or Internet) are copyrighted, meaning that you probably do not have the right to reproduce that image. The entire issue of what you may legally do with copyrighted digital materials is one you may want to discuss with your teacher or reference librarian.

That said, there are places on the Internet where users are given permission to copy images for educational purposes or personal use. See, for example, the policy of the Fine Arts Museum of San Francisco (http://famsf.org) and the policy of Art Images for College Teaching (http://mcad.edu/AICT/ html/index.html). As a precaution, always be sure to review the guidelines for usage before you download any image.

To download an image from the Internet, right click on the image (if you are using a PC) or click and hold down your mouse button (if you are using a Mac). You will find an option that says "Save image as..." Select this option and either accept the default name or give it a name of your own to help you with your archiving.

As you acquire images, it is a good idea to file them in a similar way to the text files you have archived. You might place the images in an Image folder—a subdirectory of the original Theater History Paper. Within the Image folder you can create subdirectories of images, for example: Architecture, Costumes, Portraits of Actors. At some point, you may wish to have visual access to your collection of images on file—here a "shareware" program can help. ThumbsPlus, a shareware image-sorting program that allows you to attach bibliographic information, is available for a trial use from http://www.cerious.com.

Just as you record text sources in a bibliography, you need to note the source of any graphic images you acquire. A simple way to do this is to keep a log in each image subdirectory in which you note the name of the file and any bibliographic information.

Storage Media

Protect yourself from the eventual failure of your computer hard drive by routinely backing up all of your documents to another disk or disks. One of the physical problems with collecting information, particularly graphic files, is that the material you collect takes up disk space. Using high-capacity storage devices (such as Zip disks or rewriteable CDs) allows you to store a great deal more information than a regular 3.5-inch floppy. Check with your academic computing lab to see if they have mechanisms and recommendations for storing large amounts of material.

C H A P T E R **5**

Reporting Your Research

 Fair use and the copyright law

Provide the source for every idea or fact

The material you find electronically was put there by someone, and you are legally and morally required to give appropriate credit—just as you do for other sources of information. You will notice on many Websites a line from the author granting permission to reproduce the material for personal use—but you still have to give that author credit. And, in fact, you want the authority of the source as support for the quality of your research and the legitimacy of your conclusions. As with print sources, give as complete a description as you can, so the reader of your paper can consult your sources firsthand if desired.

Withstand the temptation to keep huge chunks of material that you found in their original form. It is tempting—particularly because everything is already typed! Know that the penalty for plagiarism is severe (failure of the course or expulsion from college), and you're likely to be discovered, since your instructor has the same Internet access as you. Some instructors, in fact, are now requiring their students to print all their sources of information and submit them with their paper.

Be sure that your thoughts dominate the report. Your paper is your interpretation of what you have found—supported by the facts and opinions you cite. In other words, don't just string your findings together without reacting to the information: Analyze and interpret the data, in a logical format, according to your sense of the most important points. Make certain that you place quotation marks around any phrases taken from another person's writing or speech, and tell where you got those phrases.

Follow the correct format

Your teacher will probably specify a format or formal writing style that is preferred for writing papers. Most teachers will recommend the *MLA Handbook for Writers of Research Papers,* 5th edition. No matter which style you use, you will need to indicate in the body of your paper where you got each fact or idea. You will also need a list of all of the sources of information presented in your report.

The format for reporting electronic resources has been evolving parallel to the popularity of the Internet and World Wide Web for research. The site for *Beyond the MLA Handbook: Documenting Electronic Sources on the Internet* by Andrew Harnack and Gene Kleppinger of Eastern Kentucky University, Richmond, KY (http://english.ttu.edu/kairos/1.2/inbox/ mla_archive.html) is an excellent resource that examines the evolving methods of citing electronic sources.

The most important guideline to abide by is that the reader of your paper should be able to find your source. If it's a source that may have been modified or deleted, it is important that you identify the date of your reading. The following formats represent the consensus of the scholars publishing on this type of documentation as of July 2000.

Citing sources at the end of your paper: Works Cited, References, or Bibliography

Note: You may either italicize or underline titles, as long as you use one format consistently throughout your paper. Indentations are five spaces. Your entire list should be double-spaced, with no extra spaces between entries. If information is not available—for example, the name of the author—just list whatever information you have, in the order given below, without blank spaces.

Stand-alone database or CD-ROM

Author (if given). "Title or heading of material
    you read." Title of the publication. Name of
    the editor, compiler or translator (if
    relevant). Publication medium. Edition,
    release or version. Place of publication: name
    of the publisher, Date of the publication.

Kael, Pauline. "Pauline Kael Review: *West Side
    Story.*" I Lost It at the Movies. Cinemania 96.
    CD-ROM. Microsoft. 1996.

Quittner, Joshua. "A Web of Uses for Spiders' Silk
    (Spiders' Silk for Soldiers?)." Newsday Index
    6 July 1991, sec. News: 10. CD-ROM. Newsday,
    1992.

"Safety Assured." Work Study 42 (Sept.-Oct. 1993).
    CD-ROM. ABI/Inform. 1995.

Online source or Website

Author or organization (if known). "Title of
    article." Title of complete work Volume number,
    issue number, or other identifying number. Date
    of publication. Number range or total number of
    pages, paragraphs, or other sections, if they
    are numbered. Date (day, month, year) of access
    <Address of Web site>.

Harrison, Mick J. "Poisoning Ourselves with Toxic
    Incinerators." Top Censored Newstories of 1994!
    Sept. 1994. (25 Aug. 1995.)
    <http://www.censored.sonoma.edu/ProjectCensored
    />.

If you reached the Web site from a link on another Web site where
readers of your paper could find additional relevant information, give the
title of that Website and the linking phrase.

Author or organization [if known]. "Title of
    article." Lkd. (abbreviation for *Linked from*)
    Title of site you linked from at Linking

phrase. Date of publication. <Address of
   Website>.

Agency for Toxic Substance and Disease Registry.
   Index. Lkd. Envirolink Library at Government.
   (6 June 1996.)
   <http://atsdr1.atsddr.cdc.gov:8080/atsdrhome.
   html>

Direct e-mail to you (not a discussion group)

Author [Title or area of expertise]. E-mail to the
   author (that's you). Date.

Young, Sally, PhD [Director of Composition, U of
   Tennessee at Chattanooga]. E-mail to the
   author. 13 May 1996.

Posting to a discussion group

Real name of author. <E-mail address of author>
   "Subject line of article." Date of posting.
   <Group to which it was sent-multiple groups
   separated by comma> via [which means by way of]
   <Where article can be retrieved> Date you
   viewed it.

Nevers, David M. <dmnevers@ix. netcom.com> "Re:
   Women's Violence against Men." 14 June 1996.
   <alt.feminism,soc.men> via <http:xp6.dejanews.
   com/getdoc.xp?recnum=....db96q3&CONTEXT=8392737
   50.20857&hitnum=56> 5 Aug. 1996.

Citing sources in the body of your paper

All the documentation styles require that you indicate indebtedness to a
source in the body of your paper while you are presenting information.
However, you don't need to clutter the body of your paper with Internet
addresses. Just give the briefest reference you can, so that interested readers
can turn to the end of your paper to find the source. When in doubt, use as

your guide the format your discipline requires for an article in a scholarly journal.

Modern Language Association (MLA) style

Parenthetical citations are used in the body of the paper to indicate the source, which is then listed at the end of the paper in the Works Cited. However, parenthetical citations require page numbers, which electronic sources do not ordinarily have. So you will not need parenthetical citations for your electronic sources. Instead, as you present information, incorporate the author or organization smoothly into your sentence.

```
Jason P. Mitchell interprets Maggie and Big Daddy
as "less sympathetic" and Brick as "more
compelling," based on Tennessee Williams's
comments in an interview published in 1955.
```

The reader of your paper could then turn to the Works Cited where you would have listed the complete reference.

```
Mitchell, Jason P. "The Artist as Critic: A
    Reconstruction of Brick Pollitt." 23 May
    1996. <http://sunset.backbone.olemiss.edu/
    %7Ejmitche/misphil.htm>.
```

Classic footnote (or endnote) style

In this style, you also use raised numbers in the body of your paper, but the numbers refer to a specific note that gives the bibliographical information plus page number—or date with a source from the Internet. With this method, you often can omit a separate bibliography; check with your teacher.

Start numbering consecutively, beginning with the number 1 after the first presentation of research information. Use a different number for each presentation of information (regardless of whether the source is the same or different). In the body of your paper, it would look like this:

```
If Morning Ever Comes, Anne Tyler's first novel,
was written when she was just twenty-two.[2]
```

Then, either at the foot of the page where you gave the information (for footnotes) or in a numerically ordered list at the end of the paper (for endnotes), provide the source of the information for each corresponding number in your paper.

[2]Random House. "About the Author." 15 June 1996. <http://www.randomhouse.com/knopf/read/ladder/tyler.html>.

R E F E R E N C E S

Gibaldi, Joseph. *MLA Handbook for Writers of Research Papers,* 5th ed.
New York: Modern Language Association, 1999.

Harnack, Andrew and Eugene Kleppinger. "Beyond the MLA Handbook:
Documenting Electronic Sources on the Internet."10 June 1996.
(19 May 1999).
<http://english.ttu.edu/ kairos/1.2/inbox/mla_archive.html>

Li, Xia and Nancy Crane. "Bibliographic Formats for Citing Electronic
Information." 29 October 1997. (19 May 1999).
<http://www.uvm.edu/~ncrane/estyles/>

Walker, Janice R. "The Columbia Guide to Online Style." 1 September
1998. (19 May 1999).
<http://www.columbia.edu/cu/cup/ cgos/idx_basic.html>

D A T A B A S E &
S E A R C H   T O O L S

Databases

Look for these in your library. They may be listed in a menu of choices on your library's home page, or they may be installed in designated computers. Some are also available in print, but the electronic versions are much faster to use. Use the searching techniques described in Chapter 3.

Indexes

Art Abstracts
Humanities Abstracts
ARTbibliographies Modern
Arts and Humanities Citation Index
Avery Index to Architectural Periodicals
Bibliography of the History of Art
International Bibliography of Theatre
MLA Bibliography
Dissertation Abstracts International

Search Engines

Metasearch engines

Metacrawler
  http://www.go2net.com
find.com
  http://find.com
Dogpile
  http://www.dogpile.com

General Search Engines

AltaVista
http://www.altavista.com
Excite
http://www.excite.com
Infoseek
http://infoseek.go.com
HotBot
http://hotbot.lycos.com
Lycos
http://www.lycos.com
Google
http://google.com
Yahoo!
http://www.yahoo.com

Search engines for image and media searches

Scournet
http://www.scournet.com
AltaVista Photo & Media Finder,
http://image.altavista.com/cgi-bin/avncgi
Yahoo! Image Surfer
http://isurf.yahoo.com

Electronic journals and magazines

ATHE_NEWS (Association for Theatre in Higher Education)
athenews@lists.wayne.edu
http://www.hawii.edu/athe

Didaskalia: Ancient Theatre Today
http://didaskalia.berkeley.edu

Early Modern Literary Studies
http://purl.oclc.org/emls/emlshome.html

OFF: The Journal of Alternative Theatre
http://www.bway.net/~skutsch/jwoodward/off.html

TPI: Theatre Perspectives International
http://www.tesser.com/tpi

Print journals with online information

American Drama
http://www.uc.edu/www/amdrama

On-Stage Studies
http://www.colorado.edu/TheatreDance/OnStage/index.html

TDR: The Drama Review
http://mitpress.mit.edu/journals/DRAM/tdr-index.html

Theatre InSight
http://www.utexas.edu/students/ti

Theater Magazine
http://www.yale.edu/drama/publications/theater

Online indexes and databases

Theatre Education Literature Review
http://www.aaae.org/theatre/thfront.html

OCLC: Online Computer Library Center
http://www.oclc.org

The OTIS Index
http://www.otis.net/index.html

Visual & Performing Arts INFOMINE
http://infomine.ucr.edu/search/artssearch.phtml

Electronic Texts

ALEX: Catalogue of Electronic Texts
http://sunsite.berkeley.edu/alex/

Comedia Text Archive
>   http://www.coh.arizona.edu/spanish/comedia

INTERNET-ON-A-DISK
>   http://www.samizdat.com

Project Gutenberg
>   http://www.promo.net/pg

THEATRALES (in French)
>   http://www.er.uqam.ca/nobel/c2545/theatral.html

I N D E X

404 error, 7

Academic computing, 4
Addresses (*see* Internet
    addresses)
Advanced searches, 21–22
Archives, 29
Arts and Humanities Citation
    Index, 13
Assessment questions, 24–25

Back button, *inside back cover*
Bandwidth, 17
BBS (bulletin board server), 27–
    28
Bibliographic databases, 12
Bookmarks, 31–32
Bookmark button, *inside back*
    cover
Break key, *inside back cover*
Browsing the Internet, 4
Bulletin board server (BBS), 27

CD-ROM, 2
    format for citing, 37
Citation indexes, 13
Citing sources, 36–39
    Footnote or endnote style for,
      39
    MLA style for, 39
.com, 6
Connecting to the Internet, 4
Copyright law, 35–36
Courtesy on the Internet, 17

Databases, 12
    bibliographic, 12
    full-text, 13
    stand-alone, 37
Dejanews, 28
Directories, 22
    of Internet addresses, 42–45
    for research, 22, 42–45
Discussion groups, 38
    format for citing, 38
Documentation of sources, 36–
    40
Domain Name system (DNS), 6
Downloading, 3

.edu, 6
e-mail (electronic mail), 3, 5,
    27–30
    format for citing, 38
    phrasing, 30
    use of, in research, 27, 30
Endnote style, 39
Error messages, 9
Escape character, 27
Exiting, 9

FAQs (frequently asked
    questions), 29
Favorites, 31–32
Flaming, 17
Footnote style, 39
Formats for documentation, 14
Forums, 27–28
    format for citing, 38

TYPING REMINDERS

Type carefully because a mistake can take you to the wrong location or to nowhere at all. If you know you typed correctly, be aware that the Internet changes rapidly. Use the directories and search engines on pages 42–45 . In general:

- Check each character before pressing Enter/Return.
- Use no spaces with Internet addresses.
- Use no period at the end (there may be a slash [/]).
- Use lowercase unless you are told that the program is "case sensitive" or you are copying an obvious capital in an Internet address.
- Use the Shift key (not the Caps Lock key) for the upper symbol on the number or punctuation keys.
- Be careful to distinguish between the letter *l* and the number *1*, the hyphen (-) and the underline (_) which is above the hyphen.
- The ~ symbol is the Spanish tilde, above the grave accent (`) at the top left of the keyboard.
- Slashes (//) are **forward** slashes, at the bottom right of the keyboard.
- The **Break** key is also called **Pause**; it's on the top right of the keyboard, above **PageUp**.
- On the Macintosh®, **Ctrl** is an open apple symbol and **Alt** is a filled-in apple symbol.
- Within Websites, you can click on "buttons" on the margins of the page you're looking at:
  Back takes you to the previous page.
  Forward takes you to the next page, but only after you've first moved bckwards.
  Reload gets the Website back on your screen.
  Bookmark saves the address of the Website to your list (also called Favorites or Hotlist).
  Home gets you to the home page of your server—your college, library, or online service.
  History lists the sites already visited.
  Stop interrupts downloading or the attempt to reach a site, necessary during a slowdown.
  The **X** or **square** in the top right-hand corner of the screen (or top-left for Mac) allows you to exit quickly—usually returning you to your home page, but sometimes signing you off.